The Three Little Pigs

Margot Zemach

The Three Little Pigs

AN OLD STORY

A Sunburst Book

Farrar, Straus and Giroux

For Addie, with love

Long ago, three little pigs lived happily with their momma pig. But the day came when their momma told them it was time for them to go out into the world. "Build good, strong houses," she said, "and always watch out for the wolf. Now goodbye, my sons, goodbye."

As the first little pig was going along, he met a man who was gathering straw. "Please, sir," he said, "give me some straw to build me a house." So the man gave him some straw and the first little pig built himself a house.

One day the wolf came knocking at his door. "Little pig, little pig," he called. "Let me come in!" But the first little pig said: "No, no, I won't let you in—not by the hair of my chinny-chin-chin."

"Well then," said the wolf, "I'll huff and I'll puff and I'll blow your house down." So he huffed and he puffed and he blew the house down, and he ate up the first little pig. Yumm-yum!

As the second little pig was going along, he met a man with a load of sticks. "Please, sir," he said, "give me some sticks to build me a house." So the man gave him some sticks and the second little pig built himself a house.

One day the wolf came knocking at his door. "Little pig, little pig," he called. "Let me come in!" But the second little pig said: "No, no, I won't let you in—not by the hair of my chinny-chin-chin."

"Well then," said the wolf, "I'll huff and I'll puff and I'll blow your house down." So he huffed and he puffed and he huffed and he puffed and he blew the house down, and he ate up the second little pig. Yumm-yum!

As the third little pig was going along, he met a man with a load of bricks. "Please, sir," he said, "give me some bricks to build me a house." So the man gave him some bricks and the third little pig built himself a good, strong house.

One day the wolf came knocking at his door. "Little pig, little pig," he called. "Let me come in!" But the third little pig said: "No, no, I won't let you in—not by the hair of my chinny-chin-chin."

"Well then," said the wolf, "I'll huff and I'll puff and I'll blow your house down." So he huffed and he puffed and he huffed and he puffed . . .

and he huffed and he puffed, but he just *couldn't* blow the house down!

This made the wolf angry, but he only said, "Little pig, I know where there's a field of turnips."

"Oh, where?" asked the third little pig.

"Right down the road," said the wolf. "I'll come for you at ten o'clock tomorrow morning, and we'll go together."

The next morning the little pig got up at nine o'clock and hurried to the turnip field. He was back safe in his house when the wolf came knocking.

"Little pig," said the wolf. "It's time to go."

"Oh, I already got myself a nice basket of turnips," the little pig said. This made the wolf very angry, but he just said, "Little pig, I know where there's a big apple tree."

"Oh, where?" asked the little pig.

"Across the meadow," said the wolf. "I'll come for you tomorrow at nine o'clock. We'll go together."

The next morning the little pig got up at eight o'clock. He was busy picking apples when he saw the wolf coming. "Here's an apple for you!" the little pig called, and he threw it so far the wolf had to chase after it. Then the little pig climbed down and ran away.

As soon as the little pig was safe in his house, the wolf came knocking. "Little pig," he said, "tomorrow there's going to be a fair in town. I'll come for you at eight o'clock."

The next morning the little pig got up at seven o'clock and hurried to the fair, where he had a good time, until he saw the wolf coming. The little pig jumped into a barrel to hide. But the barrel fell over and rolled down the hill, faster and faster, straight toward the wolf—and it knocked him down!

The little pig was cooking himself a big pot of soup when the wolf came banging on his door. "Little pig," he called, "I didn't see you at the fair."

"Oh, but I saw you," said the little pig. "I was riding home in the barrel that knocked you down." This made the wolf really angry, much angrier than before.

"Little pig!" he roared. "I've had enough of your tricks. Now I'm coming to get you." The wolf leaped onto the little pig's roof and he threw himself down the little pig's chimney, and he fell right into the pot of soup and was cooked.

That night, the third little pig had wolf soup for supper. Yumm-yum!